What are
stratus clouds?

Lynn Peppas

Clouds Close-Up

Author
Lynn Peppas

Publishing plan research and development
Sean Charlebois, Reagan Miller
Crabtree Publishing Company

Editorial director
Kathy Middleton

Editor
Reagan Miller

Proofreader
Crystal Sikkens

Photo research
Allison Napier, Samara Parent

Design
Samara Parent

Production coordinator
Samara Parent

Prepress technician
Katherine Berti

Print coordinator
Katherine Berti

Illustrations
Barbara Bedell: pages 6–7 (except water droplets)
Katherine Bert: page 7 (water droplets)

Photographs
Digital Vision: page 9 (bottom)
Shutterstock: cover, title page, pages 4, 5 (right), 8, 9 (top),
    12, 13, 14, 15, 18, 18, 21, 22, 23
Thinkstock: contents page, pages 10, 17, 20
Wikimedia Commons: Fir0002/Flagstaffotos: page 5 (left);
    Benutzer: LivingShadow: page 16

Library and Archives Canada Cataloguing in Publication

Peppas, Lynn
    What are stratus clouds? / Lynn Peppas.

(Clouds close-up)
Includes index.
Issued also in electronic format.
ISBN 978-0-7787-4476-4 (bound).--ISBN 978-0-7787-4481-8 (pbk.)

    1. Stratus--Juvenile literature. 2. Weather--Juvenile literature.
I. Title. II. Series: Peppas, Lynn. Clouds close-up.

QC921.43.S8P47 2012   j551.57'6   C2012-901516-4

Library of Congress Cataloging-in-Publication Data

CIP available at Library of Congress

Crabtree Publishing Company

www.crabtreebooks.com   1-800-387-7650

Printed in Canada/042012/KR20120316

Published in Canada
Crabtree Publishing
616 Welland Ave.
St. Catharines, Ontario
L2M 5V6

Published in the United States
Crabtree Publishing
PMB 59051
350 Fifth Avenue, 59th Floor
New York, New York 10118

Published in the United Kingdom
Crabtree Publishing
Maritime House
Basin Road North, Hove
BN41 1WR

Published in Australia
Crabtree Publishing
3 Charles Street
Coburg North
VIC 3058

Contents

What are clouds?

Look up in the sky. What do you see? On most days, you will spot clouds in the sky. Clouds are made up of tiny drops of water or little pieces of ice.

One picture shows clouds that bring rain and the other shows clouds that bring fair weather. Do you know which is which?

Weather watcher

Weather changes from day to day. Some days are sunny and warm. Other days can be rainy and cool. Different clouds bring different kinds of weather.

The water cycle

The **water cycle** describes the movement of water on, in, and above the earth. Clouds are an important part of this cycle. Follow the arrows to learn more about water's amazing journey!

Heat from the Sun warms the water in oceans, lakes, rivers, and even puddles!

*The heat from the Sun causes the water to **evaporate**, or change into **water vapor**.*

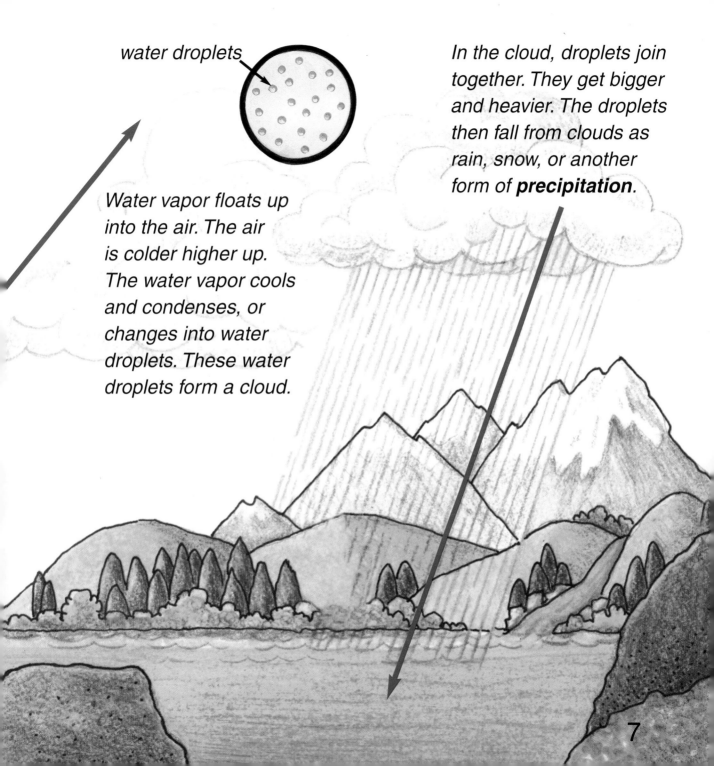

water droplets

In the cloud, droplets join together. They get bigger and heavier. The droplets then fall from clouds as rain, snow, or another form of **precipitation**.

Water vapor floats up into the air. The air is colder higher up. The water vapor cools and condenses, or changes into water droplets. These water droplets form a cloud.

Cloud Names

stratus clouds

cumulus clouds

There are three main kinds of clouds—**cirrus**, **stratus**, and **cumulus** clouds. They were named more than 200 years ago by a man named Luke Howard. Howard named the clouds using **Latin** words that were based on their shape.

8

cirrus clouds

Stratus means "layer," cumulus means "heap" or "pile," and "cirrus" means "curls of hair."

Do you think the names of the clouds match their shapes?

How high?

Clouds form at different heights in the sky. Some clouds form high in the sky. Other clouds form low in the sky. There are three words used to describe the height of a cloud in the sky. From lowest to highest, they are strato, alto, and cirro.

Cloud levels

High clouds

Cloud names that begin with cirro are the highest clouds in the sky.

Middle clouds

Clouds in the middle of the sky have names that start with "alto."

Low clouds

Clouds that form low in the sky have "strato" in their name.

above 18,000 feet (5,486 meters)

6,500 feet (1,981 meters) to 18,000 feet (5,486 meters)

up to 6,500 feet (1,981 meters)

Cloud types

High clouds

*cirrus
cirrostratus
cirrocumulus*

Middle clouds

*altostratus
altocumulus*

Low clouds

*stratus
stratocumulus
nimbostratus*

11

Cirrus and cumulus clouds

Sometimes cirrus clouds are called mares' tails. A mare is a female horse. Do you think this is a good name for this cloud?

Cirrus clouds are thin, wispy, and white. They form very high in the sky where the air is cold. Cirrus clouds are made up of ice crystals. Strong winds blow the clouds, causing their wispy look. Cirrus clouds are a sign that the weather will change within one day.

Cumulus clouds

Cumulus clouds have bright fluffy tops and flat gray bottoms. They are made up of water droplets. Cumulus clouds are called "fair-weather" clouds because they are a sign of good weather.

cirrus clouds

cumulus clouds

Clouds made up of ice crystals have feathery edges.

Clouds made up of water droplets have sharp edges.

Stratus clouds

Stratus clouds can cover the sky like a thick gray blanket. They form a low layer that can cover the entire sky. Stratus clouds can bring **drizzle**, or light rain, when it is warm and snow when it is cold.

More about stratus clouds

Stratus clouds are the lowest clouds in the sky. Sometimes precipitation does not fall and the sky is **overcast**. Overcast means that it blocks a bit of the Sun's light.

Altostratus clouds

Altostratus clouds are gray or bluish-gray in color. They are a thin, unbroken blanket of cloud. Sometimes you can see the Sun through them, but it will look **hazy**. They are made of water droplets or ice crystals depending on how cold the air is around them.

Altostratus weather

Different kinds of clouds mean different kinds of weather. Altostratus clouds mean a lot of precipitation is coming soon. Sometimes altostratus clouds bring drizzle.

Cirrostratus clouds

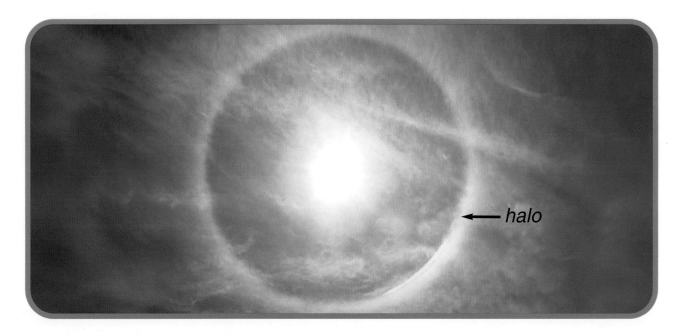

halo

Cirrostratus clouds are found high in the sky. Like all stratus clouds, they form in a smooth sheet or layer. Cirrostratus clouds are made of ice crystals. They are so thin that light from the Sun or Moon passes through the clouds. When this happens, a **halo**, or ring, forms around the Sun or Moon.

Cirrostratus weather

Cirrostratus clouds are a sign that the weather is changing. Cirrostratus clouds are usually seen 12 to 24 hours before a rainstorm or snowstorm.

Fog

Fog is a type of stratus cloud. It is a collection of water droplets that form on the ground. Water droplets form when cool air condenses the water vapor near the ground.

Sight-seeing

Fog makes it hard to see for long distances. That is because of all the water droplets in the air. In fog you can see less than 3,300 feet (1000 m) away.

Make your own fog

You will need a parent, teacher, or caregiver to help with this experiment.

Materials:

very hot water

large glass jar

ice cubes

strainer

black construction paper

Directions:

1. Have an adult fill the glass jar with hot water. Let it stand for one minute. Empty the water and put one inch (2.5 centimeters) of hot water in the bottom of the jar.

2. Place the strainer at the top of the jar.

3. Place three ice cubes in the strainer.

4. Hold the black construction paper behind the jar.

Get ready for fog!

What you see is like the water cycle. Water that is heated evaporates, or changes from its liquid form to a gas form and rises upward. The warm air reaches the ice cubes and cools. The air condenses and forms a cloud of fog!

Words to know

cirrus Thin, high-forming clouds made of ice crystals
cumulus Puffy, white clouds
drizzle A light, misty rain
evaporate To change from a liquid to a gas
halo A circle of light that surrounds something
hazy Blurry, or not clear
Latin An old language that was used thousands of years ago
overcast When a lot of gray clouds block some of the Sun's light
precipitation Rain, snow, or hail that falls from clouds to the earth
stratus Thick, gray, low-forming clouds
water cycle Describes how water moves between Earth's surface and the sky
water vapor Water that has changed from a liquid to a gas
weather What the air is like at a certain time and place

Index

Learning more

Books:
What is Climate? by Bobbie Kalman. Crabtree Publishing Company, 2012.
Changing Weather: Storms by Bobbie Kalman. Crabtree Publishing Company, 2006.
The Weather by Deborah Chancellor. Crabtree Publishing Company, 2010.

Websites:
http://eo.ucar.edu/webweather/cloudhome.html
www.weatherwizkids.com
www.northcanton.sparcc.org/~elem/interactivities/clouds/cloudsread.html